Two Birds
...and a MOOSE

by
James Preller

illustrated by
Abigail Burch

Ready-to-Read

Simon Spotlight
New York   London   Toronto   Sydney   New Delhi

SIMON SPOTLIGHT
An imprint of Simon & Schuster Children's Publishing Division
1230 Avenue of the Americas, New York, New York 10020
This Simon Spotlight edition August 2024
Text copyright © 2024 by James Preller
Illustrations copyright © 2024 by Abigail Burch
All rights reserved, including the right of reproduction in whole or in part in any form.
SIMON SPOTLIGHT, READY-TO-READ, and colophon are registered trademarks of Simon & Schuster, LLC.
Simon & Schuster: Celebrating 100 Years of Publishing in 2024
For information about special discounts for bulk purchases, please contact Simon & Schuster Special Sales at 1-866-506-1949 or business@simonandschuster.com.
The Simon & Schuster Speakers Bureau can bring authors to your live event. For more information or to book an event contact the Simon & Schuster Speakers Bureau at 1-866-248-3049 or visit our website at www.simonspeakers.com.
Manufactured in the United States of America 0724 LAK • 10 9 8 7 6 5 4 3 2 1
Library of Congress Cataloging-in-Publication Data
Names: Preller, James, author. | Burch, Abigail, illustrator. Title: Two birds . . . and a moose / by James Preller ; illustrated by Abigail Burch. Description: New York: Simon Spotlight, 2024. | Series: Ready-to-read | Summary: A determined moose attempts to bounce, float, and climb to new heights while two birds observe from their perch. Identifiers: LCCN 2023051921 (print) | LCCN 2023051922 (ebook) | ISBN 9781665948791 (hardcover) | ISBN 9781665948784 (paperback) | ISBN 9781665948807 (ebook) Subjects: CYAC: Moose—Fiction. | Birds—Fiction. | Determination—Fiction. | LCGFT: Animal fiction. | Picture books. Classification: LCC PZ7.P915 Tw 2024 (print) | LCC PZ7.P915 (ebook) | DDC [E]—dc23 | LC record available at https://lccn.loc.gov/2023051921 | LC ebook record available at https://lccn.loc.gov/2023051922

Two birds in a tree.

One red, one blue.

BOING!
BOING!
BOING!

And a moose!

Bye, Moose.

Two birds on a wire.

And a balloon . . .

Up and up, higher and higher into the sky.

Down goes Moose.

Down, down . . . *SPLAT!*

Almost there!

One moose in a tree.

THE END